Firsts
AND LASTS

Firsts
AND LASTS

ANNETTE LYON

Also by Annette Lyon

NOVELS
Lost Without You
At the Water's Edge
House on the Hill
At the Journey's End
Spires of Stone
Tower of Strength
Band of Sisters
Band of Sisters: Coming Home
The Newport Ladies Book Club: Paige
The Newport Ladies Book Club: Ilana's Wish
Tying the Knot
A Portrait for Toni

NOVELLAS
An Unexpected Proposal
Chasing Tess
Golden Sunrise
Chocolate Obsessed
War of Hearts
Between the Lines
A Taste of Home
Perfectly Imperfect

NONFICTION
There, Their, They're:
A No-Tears Guide to Grammar from the Word Nerd
Chocolate Never Faileth
Done & Done:
The Power of Accountability Partnering for Reaching Your Goals
(with Luisa M. Perkins)

Chapter One

D ani stood on the sidewalk, looking up the grand staircase outside the Metropolitan Museum of Art. Although she'd seen the building several times during her six months in Manhattan, she'd never really stopped to look at it, and she'd never been inside.

People rushed past her as they went their different ways up and down Fifth Avenue. She could easily identify the residents over the tourists. Real New Yorkers moved with a quick, no-nonsense stride. Businesswomen in dress pants and jackets often walked in sneakers. Dani had learned that they kept high heels in their purses or at the office to switch into after they got to work. She could hear the whoosh and honks of traffic behind her.

Several strollers passed, making Dani step out of the way. Some were pushed by mothers, others by nannies. Dani glanced at a pair of women pushing strollers with toddlers about the same age. They chatted and laughed— and looked completely at home.

I want that—to feel at home here. But she didn't, not after six months, not after experiencing a New York winter turned to spring, and not now that this was the official first day of summer, either. By some miracle, the humidity was low, but the air was hot, alleviated slightly by a cool breeze blowing down the corridors of the streets as if through a canyon. Standing so close to Central Park, she could feel the coolness there like an oasis beckoning her to come in and escape the heat.

She still related better to the other people walking the streets, the ones who were obviously tourists. They had that starry-eyed gaze as they consulted maps—whether on paper or on their cell phones—and argued about whether to see the Statue of Liberty or go to the top of the Empire State Building. They were the ones whose chins often tilted back as their eyes searched for the tops of the skyscrapers.

Dani had done that too when she'd first arrived. So maybe she wasn't exactly a tourist anymore, not in the typical sense. She could get around without a map. She knew which trains to take to get from point A to point B.

But so much was still foreign, even the sounds. She hadn't quite gotten used to having the constant energy and buzz of a city that never slept. The busiest street back home in Pekin, Illinois, paled in comparison to the sea of yellow taxis and buses passing her now.

She'd come here to pursue her dreams of performing on Broadway, yet here she was a step away from leaving it all.

Her mind and heart warred against each other, and had for weeks. Her mind—which tended to echo her mother's sentiments—insisted that she'd given it her best shot and needed to go back home. She should settle down into "real" life. But her heart cried out that six months wasn't enough, that she needed more time to give this dream thing a shot. That she was good and just needed to get in front of the right directors and producers at the right time, with the right project, to get her big break. Her mother wanted her to return home, find a man, have a litter of babies, and spend the rest of her life doing nothing more remarkable than canning peaches.

The bitter reality of having run out of money was the weight that had finally tipped the scales in the direction of the logical mind winning out over her heart. The jobs she'd found as a waitress, dishwasher, and cashier at a souvenir shop had paid her bills—barely—but they also required her to work intense hours, leaving her almost no time for auditions or callbacks. She was here, so close to her dream, but unable to grab the brass ring.

She'd been through these thoughts and arguments over and over again. Time to stop thinking about it all and just enjoy today for what it was, to fully embrace all of the sights she would see for the first—and likely last—time.

Again she raised her eyes to the top of the wide stair-case, which had students, tourists, and others walking up and down, some sitting in various spots. Her eyes stopped at the grand white building that was the Metropolitan Museum of Art—what she still called "the Met," even though she'd recently learned that New Yorkers typically thought of "the Met" as the Metropolitan Opera, and the museum as the MMA. Further evidence that she hadn't managed to fit in. She wasn't really a New Yorker.

Last month, some of the biggest celebrities in the world had gathered here for the annual fashion show. Dani wished she'd slowed her life down enough to notice it at the time, to have come up here from her apartment to watch the stars walk the red carpet in their magnificent gowns instead of merely seeing it all reported on during the morning news shows like the rest of the country.

As vast as the museum was, it seemed to be almost nestled within the greenery that was Central Park, safe and secure. From where she stood, she could feel the cooler temperature wafting off the park, a respite in the middle of an ocean of concrete and asphalt. Dani had half a mind to go to Central Park now and wander the miles and miles of paths until she got lost, just so she could say she'd seen everything there was to see inside it—every statue, bridge, path, and street performer. The zoo. The restaurants. The open-air theater. She could see herself spending hours at the Conservatory Garden alone. Maybe tomorrow.

Today, she'd give her time to the Met. The MMA, she corrected herself. She'd heard that a person could spend a week or more in there and still not see everything, but she'd do her best to see as much as she could today. She had too many other things on her first-and-last list to be able to give more than one day to it.

"Gorgeous, isn't it?" a deep voice said beside her. "Going to the museum today?"

Dani startled and turned to her right to see a man somewhere in his upper twenties grinning at her. "Do I— know you?"

Maybe she'd met this guy somewhere and didn't remember. They could have crossed paths at an audition or something. He couldn't be from one of the awful cattle calls she'd been in; she'd remember every face she'd ever seen during those.

One thing she'd learned during her time here was that the people were far friendlier than the New Yorker stereotype suggested. But that didn't mean they struck up conversations with total strangers on busy sidewalks.

"No, I don't believe we've met," he said, holding out a hand. "Mark Potter. No relation to Harry."

Dani's eyebrows went up, and she almost laughed. He was funny, and he didn't seem like the Ted Bundy type. Before she could speak, he went on.

"And yes, I actually have been asked that, more than once." He looked at his hand, still held out to shake hers.

She eyed it. Maybe she looked like a gullible tourist, and this guy was going to try to rip her off with some trick. He seemed a little too nice, a little too sure of himself. But she found herself reaching out to shake his hand anyway. There couldn't be any harm in that, surely.

"Nice to meet you . . . Mark."

It was his turn to raise his eyebrows, as if he'd caught how she'd deliberately not said *her* name. As they shook hands, his was warm and his grip firm but not hard.

I could get used to holding that hand, she thought, then immediately snapped herself out of the fantasy and slipped her hand away.

Mark pointed up the stairs at the Met. "You going inside?"

Should she tell the truth and risk having a potential creeper following her around, or should she hedge and lose him? Maybe she could grab a taxi and have it drive around for a while until he was gone.

Except his warm eyes kept drawing her gaze, and he seemed to be sincerely interested in her response. And, if she was being entirely honest with herself, she wouldn't mind having company for this first-and-last stop.

She found herself nodding. "Yeah," she said. "I've never been inside, which is crazy."

"Me, neither. Crazy, especially considering that I've lived here for five years. I guess it's easy to put off seeing the sights when you're right among them."

"It really is," she said, still hedging, not saying how long she'd been here. He was right, though; she'd grown up not far from Chicago, and while she'd visited the city a few times, she'd never seen the Frank Lloyd Wright home or Wrigley Field. She'd seen the Trump Tower in Manhattan, but not the one a few hours from home. She'd done the same thing in college; she'd attended Arizona State but had never managed to visit the O.K. Corral to the south or the Grand Canyon to the north. So odd how that worked.

She glanced over at Mark, deciding what to say. She wasn't a tourist, but she wasn't a local, either. Not really. But today of all days, she didn't want to be seen as an outsider.

"So what are you doing here?" she finally asked. "Visiting the Met for the first time too?"

"If you don't mind the company." He grinned, something that made her stomach flip deliciously. He cocked his head as if awaiting her answer, and a cowlicked piece of hair fell onto his forehead.

She sensed something else behind his smile, another emotion she couldn't pin down. It intrigued her. Maybe a couple of hours with this guy would tell her what that was all about. Besides, the Met had to be one of the safest places in the City, with all the security that had to be in there. She could ditch him later if she needed to. And she could definitely find worse things to do with her day than spend it with a hot guy.

"Sure," she finally said. "I'm hoping to see the American Wing first, if that's all right with you."

"Sounds good to me." He turned toward the stairs, and she started up them at his side as he went on. "I looked at the directory once and had no idea how I'd pick where to start. Figured I'd get here one day."

"And it only took you five years," she said, half teasing.

"Sort of," he said, jogging up the steps beside her. "I was raised in the Hudson Highlands, an hour's drive or so, depending on traffic. I came into the city a few times growing up—family outings, school trips, that kind of thing. But the one year our class had a field trip to the museum, I had my tonsils out. My parents were always attending symphonies and fancy restaurants, but very few touristy areas. Dad hates those. So he always said we'd visit the MMA on a Sunday, when the crowds weren't so big." He shrugged. "That Sunday never arrived. I could list off some of the best places to eat in the city, but not a single painting I've seen inside there. Let's rectify that."

When they'd reached the top of the stairs, Mark held one of the glass doors open, and Dani went inside. Two steps in, she could already feel the history, as if it had soaked into the stone floor below her feet. In spite of herself, her head tilted back, just like a tourist, so she could take in the tall walls that rose to meet arches. The lobby alone looked like a cathedral, only with gargantuan flower arrangements that were works of art themselves. It all gave her half a mind to shush the people milling about. She could have stayed there all day, enjoying the vast foyer.

At the ticket counter, Mark paid for two and handed Dani her ticket before she could object. She took it from him, their fingers grazing. A zip of electricity went up her arm.

"Thanks." She should have said more—how she was running low on funds, which was why she was leaving, so she appreciated the gesture even more. But the single word was all she could manage.

"No problem," Mark said as he unfolded the pamphlet he'd been given and found the museum map, which he examined.

"I hear the restaurant somewhere over . . . here"—he pointed to the map that looked to be past a long gallery of sculptures—"is excellent. Oh, but I have a better idea for lunch—the best hot dog stand ever. It's not too far from here."

"Sounds good to me," Dani said. You couldn't live in the city long without expecting to walk blocks and blocks every day. A short trip to a food stand sounded good.

Plus, after seeing how much Mark had paid for the two of them to get in, she was more than happy to have a cheap lunch—assuming she still wanted to hang out with this guy in a few hours. One thing she'd learned during her time here was that street vendors' unhealthy food was far cheaper than groceries and far easier to get home than schlepping bags of food for blocks and blocks to cook in the tiny apartment kitchen.

"This guy's food is good," Mark promised. He rolled his eyes like a puppy in ecstasy. "Heaven on a bun, I promise."

"Let's do it," Dani said. "After we go through the American Wing, at least. We can come back to go through more of the museum after that."

"Perfect," Mark said. "Lead on."

They meandered through hallways and climbed stairs that looked old; Dani wished she could put her hand against the walls and feel the history inside them. She would have loved to know what these walls had seen and heard over the years. They reached the American Wing, where, to her surprise, the walls weren't white, but pinky salmon.

"Huh. Not what I was expecting," she said, looking about. But soon her attention was diverted from the color of the walls to the paintings hanging on them.

She'd seen many in textbooks and elsewhere over the years, but these were the originals. Many were downright huge compared to the inches-wide images she'd become accustomed to—some were taller than she was and two or more yards across. Others would have taken up a whole wall of her bedroom back home.

They wandered through the maze of the gallery, somehow staying side by side the entire time, their arms almost brushing each time they moved from one painting to another. Dani was used to friends and family laughing at her insistence on stopping at every display at a museum to really appreciate it and even read the signs. Her older sister insisted that going to a museum with Dani was seventy-five percent an exercise in waiting for her. But even though Mark didn't stop to read as much as she did, he seemed happy to move at her pace.

They gazed at each painting, and only after spending enough time to truly appreciate the work did they make a move to continue to the next. Dani found the relaxed pace oddly refreshing—no pressure to hurry up and move. She'd thought she was the only person in the world who took so long in museums.

Eventually they reached an area that must have belonged to a different wing, because she immediately recognized European works, especially several paintings in one room. Only one painter she knew of used those contrasting browns and whites and worked that way with light and shadow, along with those big ruffed collars on his subjects.

"Rembrandt," she said in awe.

"Wow," Mark said, following her. Standing several feet back, Dani studied one painting, amazed at how lifelike the ruff looked—she couldn't make out individual brushstrokes. Hands behind her back so she wouldn't accidentally touch anything, she stepped closer. But she still wasn't close enough to see the small details. She took another step closer still. Another. And that's when Mark tapped her arm.

"Uh, Dani?"

"Yeah?" she said absently, glad to finally be close enough to see the brushstrokes—twelve inches away at most.

Instead of Mark replying, a different, somewhat nasal voice did. "Miss?"

Dani turned to see who was addressing her. A security guard stood there, rocking back and forth from heel to toe. "The cameras just took a picture of you." He looked both serious and amused. But his meaning didn't register.

"Excuse me?"

He nodded at the Rembrandt. "You were too close. The security cameras took a picture of you in case you damaged the painting. You'd better stay back."

"Oh." Dani deliberately took two long strides backward, putting several feet between her and any painting. Any chance of seeing Rembrandt's individual strokes was gone. "Better?"

The security guard didn't even answer. He just walked off.

"Didn't expect that," Mark whispered with a chuckle. "Had I known I was inviting myself to come along with someone who is practically a felon . . ." He shook his head.

"Oh, please." Dani slapped his arm playfully and laughed as she headed to the next painting, another Rembrandt. "Really, how do they expect anyone to appreciate the work if we don't get to actually *look* at it? Three feet away is too far; that painting looked just as it did in my humanities textbook in college. But up close—that was seriously cool."

Mark put his hands in his pockets and stopped by her, admiring the next piece. "I dare you to do it again."

She raised her eyebrows. "Yeah, no," she said, unable to hide a smile. "I have no desire to have my face sent to security or for me to be escorted out for endangering a priceless work of art." Dani looked away, because eying him was quickly becoming a dangerous act. She could have sworn he got better-looking with each glance. She studied the painting in front of her, even though her mind was now elsewhere.

You can't let yourself get hung up on some guy you don't even know, she reminded herself. *Not when you're about to move a thousand miles away.*

"But I have no regrets about getting that close—once—if that's what you're asking," She held up her index finger to emphasize the point.

Mark didn't so much as look at her when he spoke next, but he did lean close and whisper in her ear, giving her a hint of his musky cologne. "I double-dog dare you."

At his nearness, Dani's knees threatened to give way, but she wouldn't let him see that. Wanting to smell him again, she leaned

9

in—slowly, to prolong the moment—and whispered her reply in his ear. "Not. On. Your. Life."

She sauntered off, and she couldn't help feeling a bit of a thrill when he grinned and followed behind. After a few more rooms, they reached a corridor that marked the end of this particular wing.

They headed down a staircase, with Mark ahead of her. At the bottom of the wooden steps, he paused and looked back.

"Time for hot dogs?" he asked. "Or do you want to go see some Egyptian mummies or maybe the Ancient Near Eastern Art? African? The Costume Institute?"

"I thought you didn't know much about the museum," Dani said, raising one eyebrow. Under normal circumstances, she would have preferred to stay in the museum all day, but she found herself saying yes to lunch—and meaning it. "But a hot dog sounds perfect about now," she said, even though she'd already had half a dozen in the last week.

Chapter Two

They walked down Fifth Avenue, chatting about the museum and how they really should have gone before, although truth be told, Mark was rather glad that his first introduction to the MMA was with Dani.

Approaching a good-looking, unknown woman had never been part of Mark's MO. For that matter, he'd never done it until today. But today, he'd needed a break from everything. As of this morning, he'd had another flop of an audition, racked up with all the others he'd thought had gone so well but had still yielded rejections.

So he'd tucked his oboe case into his backpack then headed to the park. His original intention was to get *away* from the City, and the park was about the best he could do without leaving the island. He missed his family's house back in Cold Spring, with its aging shade trees, green bushes, and flowers in a thousand varieties and colors. They'd be in their prime about now, mid-June: after budding and blooming but before the weather got too hot.

Dani talked about her home in Illinois, a town much different from one he'd ever lived in, surely. He couldn't quite imagine what living in the Midwest would be like, with its rolling plains and cornfields.

"I'm glad I came to New York," she said. "But I do miss home."

Mark found himself nodding. "I totally get that." He missed home too, in a lot of ways. He didn't want to go back, though, not until he had something to show for his efforts. This morning, he'd failed again. He'd come to the park—and then to the museum—to shake off the voice of his father, which always set up shop and lived in his head, whispering about how he'd failed again and always would be a loser.

Oboe performance? Really, son? That's ridiculous. Don't go studying music and then, when you can't support yourself, come limping home, expecting to stay in your old room.

In some ways, his father had a point, Mark supposed. Had he picked one of the STEM majors, he could have been making money at some big technology company or something by now instead of serving tables, eking out a living, barely able to pay rent, always hoping that the next audition was the one. He managed to make ends meet by playing freelance gigs like weddings and corporate parties, sometimes on the piccolo or bassoon—instruments he could play that weren't as common.

He'd walked past several groups of children at various statues, and as they'd played tag around the figures in the *Alice in Wonderland* statue, he'd noticed the magic in their eyes that always seemed accompany children's play.

Just as Mark's doubts had come to a crescendo, he'd left the park and reached the sidewalk. Instead of hailing a cab as intended, he'd spotted Dani at the base of the stairs. She'd stood there, looking up at the museum as if it held some last scrap of hope for her. That expression was exactly how he felt.

It was also why he'd suddenly found himself walking up to her and acting so entirely out of his comfort zone. If she brushed him off, so be it; he'd go inside and visit the museum alone. If he got to meet that beautiful woman on top of it all, so much the better.

The worst that could happen was being rejected, right? And that had already happened today. So he'd gone over and found himself talking to a perfect stranger—and connecting with her so completely in almost no time at all. The beautiful woman had turned out to be intelligent and witty and fun and so much more.

Now, as they walked down the street, he couldn't believe that two hours before, they'd never laid eyes on each other. He glanced down, where her arms swayed with each step. Their hands were so close that they might as well be touching. He could slip his hand around hers without much trouble . . . but how would she react?

And why did he suddenly care so much about that?

"We really should go back there someday," he said, breaking the silence that had consumed them both for the last moment or two.

She nodded but then shrugged. "I doubt I ever will." Her voice held a tinge of melancholy.

Never go back to the museum now that they'd just experienced a taste of? That made no sense. He stopped at the corner to wait for the light to change. "I thought you liked it."

"Oh, I did. A lot. And I'd love to see every last piece of art in there. If E. L. Konigsburg's book is accurate, there's a whole section with antique furniture." She smiled dreamily. "I'd like to see it and imagine sleeping in one of those beds like the kids in her book. Have you read it?"

"I read about Mrs. Basil E. Frankweiler and her mixed-up files over and over again in fourth grade. Even did an oral book report about it," Mark said. "I heard that the gift shop sells copies of the book. Maybe we'll make it that far another time." He left the idea hanging in the air, hoping she'd pick up on it and give him the chance to see her again. Maybe let him buy her a souvenir on their second date to remind her of their sort-of first date. And maybe they'd arrange more dates. Together, they could see the whole museum—and then experience other parts of the city neither had seen yet.

But then the signal changed, and Dani headed across the street without answering. Mark followed, but he wasn't about to be swayed by her attempt to dodge the topic.

"So, Dani . . . why won't you go back?" he asked, catching up to her through the push of the lunch crowd.

They walked down the street again, but she stopped and looked at a store. Mark had been paying so much attention to her and his thoughts that he hadn't noticed where they were until she'd stopped: the legendary FAO Schwarz toy store.

She pointed at the glass doors, where a man wearing a toy soldier's uniform "guarded" the entrance. "Ever been in there?" Her voice wasn't as strong as before. Something was bothering her, and Mark was determined to find out what.

"A few times, but not recently," he said. "Let's go in and walk around. It's pretty cool."

"Nah. I'm good, thanks." She shook her head and kept walking, heading away from the park, toward Madison Avenue.

Maybe she was tired of his company or thought he was a "creeper," as his roommate Brian's girlfriend called guys who made her skin crawl. Should he let her walk off alone? Say good-bye? Not without getting her number.

With determination, Mark strode along in step with her. "Let's get some lunch at that hot dog place I told you about. It's just a few blocks away," he said with a southeastward nod. "On me."

At last Dani slowed from her quick steps to a stroll and then stopped altogether, seeming to consider his offer. "Of course. Sorry I'm distracted. I really am starving."

Mark led the way, and while he was enjoying himself, walking along with a pretty, smart girl, he could sense that her mood had continued to shift.

And he was quite sure that it wasn't only because she needed lunch.

Chapter Three

Dani asked for her hot dog to be plain except for a little ketchup. Judging by the vendor's reaction, one would have thought she'd requested the world to be made flat. He gave Mark an approving nod after he ordered his with the works. Mustard and relish and who knew what else smothering the poor hot dog. Another way she differed from a native.

Lunches in hand, they strolled along the street. Somehow they ended up at the south end of Central Park again. Mark must have planned their path; she hadn't really paid attention to where they were going. But when she noted a free bench under a shady tree, she was glad they'd backtracked.

She sat down, and Mark joined her on the other side of the bench. She sort of wished he were sitting closer, but as soon as the thought crossed her mind, she mentally laughed at herself.

She hardly knew this guy. But she'd already taken him out of the Ted Bundy category; since leaving the museum, he'd had plenty of opportunities to pull something and had been nothing other than a gentleman. A gentleman she could relate to and laugh with, and who really did know about the best hot dog stand ever. Her dog was so good, she couldn't help roll her eyes with pleasure, even if it did have only ketchup on it.

They sat and ate in silence for a few minutes, and during that time, she made a point of not looking at him too closely, because that would make her want to get to know him better. Just because she'd taken him out of the stalker-killer category didn't mean that she would be around long enough for him to be a real prospect. She was leaving New York. In ten days, she would fly back to the Midwest, where she'd do her best to be happy.

She took another bite of her hot dog, studiously keeping her gaze on a squirrel—and *away* from admiring how well Mark's chest and shoulders filled out his shirt.

Finished with his food, Mark crunched up his hot dog wrapper in one hand then draped the other arm across the back of the bench. "So why won't you be going back to the museum with me?"

Dani glanced at him, imagining herself scooting over and sitting in the crook of his arm, which was now so available.

Instead, she made a deliberate show of chewing to finish the bite in her mouth as she tried to come up with a way to answer his question that wouldn't make her look like a silly farm girl, even though she hadn't grown up on a farm—just near some.

She'd have to tell him about why she'd come in the first place, something she didn't exactly relish the idea of doing. She swallowed and then grabbed a napkin and wiped some ketchup from the corner of her mouth. When she couldn't stall any longer, she finally said, "You'll laugh."

"No way." Mark gave a firm shake of his head. "Come on. Tell me."

For a moment, she bit her lip and actually let herself eye him—but he was smiling back, so she couldn't take in every inch without being obvious about it. His smile was enough, though—warm and inviting . . . supportive.

"I'm a walking cliché," she warned him.

"Hey, I'm rather partial to clichés." He grinned, showing his teeth, and she couldn't help but laugh. "As they say, time will tell if the grass is always greener. And it seems that the cat's got your tongue."

She laughed. "Plus, 'There's no time like the present' and 'I'm scared out of my wits'?"

"How about 'opposites attract'?" He let that cliché sink in for a second before adding a caveat, "Of course, we aren't opposites, so that cliché stinks."

She tried to let the implication slip away, to not react to the very real attraction she felt for him and the implied attraction he felt for her, cliché or not.

He leaned forward. "Come on. Tell me."

Dani crossed her legs to stall then finally said, "Okay, fine." She took a breath and dove in. "I came here after Christmas and gave myself six months to make it into a Broadway show."

Yep, total cliché. Cat's out of the bag and all that. She hurried on to rescue what positive opinion he might have created of her.

"I don't expect to get a leading role or anything, especially starting out. But I've studied voice and dance for most of my life, and I'm a decent actress, too. I'd be happy with a chorus role and the chance to work up to bigger parts over the years. But here we are, six months later, with nothing to show for it but three jobs I've been fired from because I couldn't get a replacement while I was auditioning. So I'm heading home. My flight is in ten days. And there you go. That's why I'm not going back to the museum." She paused, waiting for the expected rolling of the eyes.

Mark didn't do any such thing. Instead, he looked genuinely interested. "And?"

Dani couldn't help but tilt her head in surprise, and a smile threatened to curl the corners of her mouth.

"*And* . . . isn't the rest obvious? I never got a part, and I'm out of money."

She'd known all of that for weeks now, but saying it aloud, hearing herself say the words, made the whole thing real and painful. And pathetic. She looked away, searching for the squirrel, but it must have run off. She shrugged. "Funny how time can go slow and so fast at the same time. When I got here in the winter, six months sounded like an eternity, and some days felt like they'd never end."

17

"Especially when you're working dead-end jobs," Mark said. He spoke as if he knew.

"What do you mean?" Dani asked, hoping against hope that maybe he didn't think she was a loser for coming to New York like some backwards hick with nothing to call her own but stars in her eyes, a girl who knew more about milking cows than the theater.

I'm not that girl.

Mark leaned back. "Let me guess what your last six months have been like."

Dani folded her arms in challenge. "Go for it."

"You've worked any job you could get to pay rent and to eat. You probably share a small apartment with several others to cut costs. Auditions and callbacks rarely fit with your work schedule, so you try to get time off, but after doing that a couple of times, your bosses have had to 'reluctantly' let you go. So you're suddenly free for auditions, but broke. And so the cycle continues."

"Exactly!" Dani said with wonder in her voice. "I've been fired three times. I've relied on temp work mostly. How did you know? Are you an actor too?" She hadn't seen him at any auditions, but that didn't necessarily mean anything; the city had a huge number of theaters, and she hadn't shown up at that many auditions, thanks to her efforts to not starve or end up homeless.

He seemed to want to hedge, his head tilting back and forth, before he answered. "I'm a musician. I play the oboe. I know all about trying to get the gigs, including auditioning to play for Broadway. Kinda sucks, doesn't it?" He took a big bite of hot dog, almost as if he were biting the head off some casting director.

Dani couldn't help but laugh; she had felt that way more times than she could count. "Then you understand why I'm going home. The six months are over, and it's past the end of chasing a dream. Time to return to reality." She brushed her palms together to rid them of crumbs from her bun.

Mark started shaking his head rapidly, but he held up a finger to tell her to wait as he chewed and swallowed. "Six months isn't enough to test a dream. Obviously, I haven't heard you sing or seen you dance or any of that. But I can recognize the fire when I see it. You've had it for a long time, haven't you?" He said it as if he could tell that she'd dreamed of making it here since she wore pigtails. "You really aren't past the end of your dream, are you?"

He probably knew her type all too well. Over the years, he'd surely seen a parade of wannabe actors and singers and dancers.

She didn't trust herself to speak at first. Then she cleared her throat and managed, "Of course the fire doesn't go out this fast. Making it has been a dream since I was five."

"And you're going to let six measly months and how many auditions—what, twelve or so?—change all that? No way."

Nine, she thought, mentally correcting him. He'd think she was a bigger loser if he knew that number, or that she'd been called back twice. This was an awfully big pond, and no one here cared that back home, she'd been an awfully big fish in a tiny pond. Out here, she might as well forget thinking of it as a pond; this was an ocean, and she was drowning.

Small or big doesn't matter; I'm not even a real fish.

She couldn't answer his question, because yes, she was going home. Yes, she was giving up on a dream she'd held for most of her life. When he didn't say anything either, a thick silence slowly descended between them. But something was held suspended in that silence, something she couldn't identify or name. A connection.

Suddenly, she didn't feel so lonely in this vast city of millions. She was going home in a matter of days—she could count it in hours, if she wanted to—and she didn't want to leave Mark behind.

Why not? I just met him. Why should I care about him? He can't possibly care about me. Her stomach went heavy and flat; she had no more appetite, even though this was, as Mark had promised, the best hot dog she'd ever tasted. She searched for something to say to end the silence; it was growing uncomfortable, and she couldn't bear to think that what she felt as a connection with Mark was nothing more than a strand of pity, even if he had hinted at attraction with his list of clichés.

After forcing a smile onto her face, Dani tucked her hair behind one ear and leaned her head against her hand, with one elbow propped onto the back of the bench. "Okay, so if six months isn't enough, enlighten me. How long did it take *you* to make it?

Chapter Four

Touché," Mark said. He looked for a trashcan for his wrapper and napkin. Dani scooted toward him—not entirely closing the distance, but shrinking it considerably.

I could get used to this, she thought. *But I shouldn't.*

"I'm serious," she said. "How long did it take you?"

He stood and tossed his trash into a nearby can as if it were a basketball hoop. "Three points," he muttered under his breath. He didn't say anything else for a moment, but he stood there with his back to Dani, as if deep in thought.

That's when she noticed a rectangular bulge in his backpack and instinctively knew what it was—his oboe. Suddenly, everything clicked into place: Why a guy like Mark was free on a random weekday instead of working. Why he encouraged her dreams as if he understood them. How he knew about lost jobs and auditions.

"You're still trying to make it," she said quietly.

"Yeah." It came out as a sigh. He nodded without turning around and shoved his hands into his pockets. "I make ends meet by doing a lot of freelance gigs." He turned around and shrugged. "Helps that I can play pretty much any woodwind. But my heart isn't with the clarinet."

"Isn't the clarinet the wimpy man's oboe?" It was her attempt at a joke, but she knew there was a kernel of truth to it. The reed and breath control required of an oboe far surpassed that of a clarinet.

The softening of muscles around his mouth hinted that she'd landed on something. Yet she recognized weariness in his voice; she'd felt the same thing every minute of every day over the last six months. Looking back at her time in the city, she had to wonder how much better off she'd have been if she'd thought to work weddings and other events like Mark had. Maybe she could have saved enough to buy herself another month.

But that was all in the past—what might have been. Right now, she wanted to see and hear the enthusiasm she'd first seen in Mark—to have the spark in his eyes return, which her words had extinguished as if she'd blown out a candle with a single breath. What could she say to fix it? Sorry wouldn't do it. Of course he knew she was sorry that they were both failures.

No. We're not both failures. He's no, anyway. His big break is around the corner.

"Play for me?" she asked quietly. She stood and reached out to touch his arm. To her relief, he didn't flinch or pull back.

He just turned his head slightly and tilted it, eyebrows raised. "Why?"

"Because I want to hear your music the way only you can play it." She hadn't planned on saying any of that, but as the words tumbled out, she meant every word. "Please?"

Mark seemed to think about it for a few seconds, but then he nodded. He sat on the bench again and unzipped his backpack, revealing the black instrument case she'd known was inside. He pulled it out it oh-so-gently, as if the instrument inside were a priceless antique. He placed the backpack on the ground near his feet, and the case on his lap. He unlatched it and opened the lid, revealing the gorgeous black-and-silver instrument that lay inside, nestled in red velvet.

One by one, he pulled out the pieces and assembled his oboe, then set the case on top of the backpack. It fell open, unheeded, as

Mark put the oboe to his lips. He placed his fingers just so on the keys, moistened the reed, breathed in, and began to play.

From the first note, it was as if he'd entered a new dimension where only he and his music existed; both his body and face took on a different look—focused concentration combined with peace and a sense of increasing joy. His shoulders and face relaxed as he swayed side to side. She knew that look; she'd felt it on the dance floor more times than she could count. The haunting notes of Ennio Mariconne's "Gabriel's Oboe" from *The Mission* floated around her—the very piece that had first made her love the oboe. Chills broke over Dani's arms and raced down her back. What were the chances that she would meet a man who played her favorite instrument so masterfully?

Every note was infused with intense emotion: melancholy and loss, with a thread of hope and joy tying it all together. More than anything else, an overarching beauty encompassed him as he moved back and forth, music flowing from his fingertips.

The moment felt holy, as if he was baring his emotions in a vulnerable, sacred way. And hers, too. Still standing, Dani found herself moving side to side as the rhythm and notes moved through her. She closed her eyes, unable to *not* move. She was a dancer; she couldn't feel such powerful music moving through her bones and expect to stand still.

Her sway evolved into a sweeping arm movement, her core contracting and releasing. Her feet soon followed, and before she knew it, she was improvising full-out with footwork, arms, her torso, even quadruple pirouettes. Her movements built from small at first to grander as the music swelled. She leapt past him, vaguely aware that Mark's focus remained entirely on his instrument; she could have been beamed to Mars, and he mightn't have noticed.

She grinned, knowing exactly what that felt like: the rush of creativity and performance, even if it was for an audience of one. She danced bigger, with turns and leaps and extensions, letting her emotions from the past six months come out in a rush, the same melancholy, loss, and hope that flowed from his oboe—the sounds that connected Dani and Mark in a way she'd never be able to put to words.

From the corner of her eye, she noticed people passing by on their way to the pond as they stopped, perhaps to watch, but she paid them no mind. Let them think what they would. She'd stopped caring what people who weren't casting directors—or her mother, at least—thought of her.

Mark's fingers stopped moving as he held a long note, then released the reed. The music stopped, and even the air seemed suddenly still. Dani's movements stopped too. She was breathing hard, wiping beads of sweat from her forehead with the back of her wrist, when a rousing applause and cheers erupted from the small gathering around them.

The noise broke the remaining spell, and she looked about. Some twenty people had stopped to watch. Many smiled as they continued on their way. Several walked over and tossed coins—in some cases, bills—into the instrument case. She bowed as if onstage, and Mark nodded deeply to acknowledge them.

After the crowd had dispersed, her heart still pounding from her sudden exertion, Dani sat close to Mark. "That was fun." She pointed at his oboe. "And that was the most beautiful thing I've ever heard. Thanks for playing for me."

Mark wore a half-smile and pointed at the instrument case. "Look. There's got to be ten or fifteen dollars in there. Not too shabby for about five minutes of work."

Dani reached down and pulled out the bills to count them—a five and four ones. "Nine bucks. And that's not counting the coins." She peered into the case with its velvet interior, where quite a few quarters and some other change lay. "Probably a few more dollars there. Good guess."

Mark shrugged, as if it was no big deal. Maybe it wasn't. But his face had suddenly darkened, and his shoulders had fallen. Dani had no idea why, but the overall effect was such a drastic change from the way he'd looked moments before while playing, that the shift made her sad—and worried.

"Did I . . . say something wrong?" she asked, scooting a couple of inches away in case she'd gotten too close.

He shook his head and licked his lips. Then he pointed at his case and shrugged. "Truth is, I've done a lot more busking than I'd care to admit. It's how I've made ends meet when I didn't have a regular job and no freelance work came my way." He leaned forward, resting his forearms on his thighs, and began rubbing his right thumb against the back of his left hand—a nervous action if ever there was one.

"I'm so sorry," Dani said. "You're so talented—and I mean that. It's crazy to think that you aren't first chair in some world-renowned symphony."

He cracked a smile at that then shook his head and laughed sardonically. "You're being very kind."

"No, I'm dead serious," Dani insisted. "I heard a lot of—"

"Here." Mark picked up the case and held it out. Dani put her hands together, palms up, and he dumped the coins into them. He took his oboe apart and went on as he put the pieces back into the case. "My father would have a field day if he ever found out that I busk pretty regularly. It's not exactly how I pictured myself making a living with my music, either, but sometimes you have to do what you have to do, and I'm not ready to give up."

He'd placed each instrument piece carefully into its spot, treating it with care. He closed the lid and latched it carefully. That oboe was his most prized possession; Dani knew it without asking.

"If you enjoy what you do, who cares?" she said. "Your dad doesn't need to ever know."

"He'll find out eventually. Somehow." Mark said it without looking at her. He slipped his oboe back into the backpack and zipped it shut.

A strained silence tried to come between them, but Dani pushed it away. "Can you live on what you make by busking?"

His pained expression softened as his mouth rounded in a smile. "Not well, but I can survive, assuming I get some freelance gigs and have several roommates to split rent and utilities with."

She could almost hear the words he wasn't saying: that his father expected him to have a "real" job, whether that meant in a restaurant cleaning tables or a place in that world-class symphony. "Then do more of it," she said. "I can tell you love busking. You make your own hours, and it would give you the flexibility to go to more and more auditions, and eventually, you will make it big, whether you're in the pit playing for *Wicked* or playing for the Metropolitan Opera or the New York Symphony Orchestra or whatever. Someday, you'll have your own concerts with an entire symphony accompanying you, like Yoyo Ma, except on oboe. And—"

Mark laughed and held up his hands in surrender. "Fine. I'll do more busking and freelance work. Happy?"

"I suppose." She nudged him with her elbow. "Come on. I'm thirsty. Let's get something to drink. My turn to show you something—my favorite smoothie place."

"Lead on," Mark said, standing. His previously somber mood seemed to have fallen from his shoulders.

"This way," she said, walking down a path that led out of the park. "I've got a handful of quarters burning a hole in my purse."

Chapter Five

Dani treated Mark to the best smoothie he'd ever had, a raspberry something or other, with several additional flavors he couldn't pin down except perhaps lime. As they sipped on their straws, talking and meandering through the hot city streets, he wished they were back at the much cooler park.

Aside from escaping the heat, he would also have been quite glad to settle down to busking again with Dani dancing to his music. Maybe she could sing along at times instead of dancing. They could come up with quite a gig, the two of them, especially if he brought a piccolo and flute to change things up.

He knew all the best spots for busking. You didn't bother with the playgrounds. That's where young kids scrambled about under the watchful eyes of their nannies, who didn't usually have cash on them and had their attention focused on their charges. Instead, he picked out spots where adults and, preferably, tourists, tended to congregate.

With their final slurps, the smoothies were gone, so they found a trashcan then headed for the nearest corner, where traffic had picked up considerably with the later hour. Rush hour would be upon them soon.

As they waited to cross, Mark pulled out his cell phone and checked the time. "It's already five?" How had the day gone so fast?

"No way," Dani said, checking the time on her pale pink wristwatch. "Time flies."

"Speaking of clichés," Mark said, and laughed. "I promised we'd get back to the museum, but I have to clock in at my latest temp job in half an hour." He tried to hide his disappointment by adding, "I'm a glamorous dishwasher."

"Don't worry about it. I totally understand," Dani said. After spending so much of their day together, he knew that she really did understand, and from firsthand experience. She turned and, walking backward, faced him as she talked. "How about you walk me to my place? It's not far." Her eyes narrowed with worry. "Unless that would make you late." She didn't have to add that doing so could cost him another not-so-glamorous job.

"I think I can manage a few blocks and still get there on time."

"Great." She jerked her head to the left, indicating which way to go, and he followed.

He mentally did the math, wondering if he really had time to walk her back to her apartment. Probably not. His boss, Andre, had promised a quick kick to Mark's butt if he arrived more than five minutes late again.

Worth the risk. This way I can see where she lives and get her number. And like she said, I can always do more busking and freelance work.

Besides, he had every intention of making good on his promise to experience the rest of the museum with her. And of getting to know her well beyond that. They'd spent most of the day together, and while they still didn't know each other particularly well, his gut told him without question that this was a woman worth getting to know. It was as if he and Dani were supposed to meet today, because what were the chances of two random strangers, with so many common interests, running into each other the way they had—and in a city of some eight million people? It was almost enough to make him believe in fate.

Which meant he had to take action, because the chances of him happening to see her again if he didn't get her number were so slim he refused to consider the idea.

"Here I am." Dani stopped at a gray, nondescript apartment building. It had the typical fire escapes and locked front door. He could have passed this very building a thousand times and never noticed it, but now he paid close attention to the cross streets and made a mental note of every detail, including the coffee shop on the corner. She held out a hand as if to shake his, the way he'd done when he'd first introduced himself. "It was great meeting you today."

He just looked at her hand. "A handshake? After Rembrandt, hot dogs, busking, and the world's best smoothies?" He smiled so she'd know he was kidding. Mostly.

"A hug?" she suggested.

He opened his arms, and she stepped into them. The embrace wasn't long, but for the few seconds it lasted, Mark had never felt more content and peaceful. He didn't want to let her go. That would mean seeing her walk away. It would mean going to work and dealing with Andre. Facing the rest of his life, which was as drab and colorless as this building. The only thing that gave life color was his music.

And now, Dani.

She gave his cheek a quick peck and pulled back. "Thanks for a great day. It's been a rough spell, and I needed it."

"Likewise." He could still feel the heat of her lips on his cheek; he wanted to reach out and take her hand to draw her back into his arms. She began digging in her purse for her key—Mark's cue to speak up or miss out on ever seeing her again. "So, could I—have your number?"

Dani's head popped up from her search, and a sadness around her eyes belied her smile. She clutched a keychain in her palm and seemed to struggle for words. Mark held his breath, not wanting to be rejected.

Please give me your number.

"Sure," she finally said. "Except that it might not be of much use to you."

Mark tried not to let disappointment register on his face. "Even though you're leaving, I'll still like to have it." He held his breath, hoping she wouldn't just dump him right there on the street, but somehow a pit began to grow in his stomach anyway.

She shrugged and played with her keys, avoiding his eyes. "Ten days . . ."

"Don't go," he said. "Or at least, let's spend your last days seeing cool stuff in the city."

She raised her eyes to his and nodded. "I'd like that. Truth is, I'll be spending the next week or so finishing off my list of firsts and lasts—all of the things I've missed out on seeing here, visiting my favorites places that I did see one last time. I want to be sure to experience as much as I can before . . ." She looked down and again fingered her keys.

"Yeah," Mark said, wishing he could change the future.

"Are you sure you want my number? Ten days isn't much."

The pit in his stomach turned to a bitter taste in his mouth. "You can't really leave," he insisted. Part of that was because of her insane dancing ability, but there was also the connection between them. Surely she'd felt it. But he went for what he guessed would be the stronger argument: what had first brought her here.

He stepped closer. "You have so much talent."

She shook her head, which made him put a hand out and cup her cheek to stop her denial. She didn't pull away. Their eyes caught, and they gazed at each other for several seconds before he found his voice. "What about everything you told me about sticking with it, that someday it'll work out?"

"That wasn't about me. It was about you." Dani reached for his hand and lowered it, now holding it in both of hers, as if bringing his idea back down to reality. "I'm out of money. I'm out of time. I—" Her voice cut off as if she wasn't sure what to say.

30

He knew the feeling. He took a step closer to her; she didn't move away. "Can I still have your number?" It was almost a whisper.

She didn't answer for a second; her eyes were shiny from unshed tears. She sniffed and then nodded, pulling her phone from her purse. "What's yours? I'll text you so you'll have mine."

Relieved at the small success, Mark rattled off his number, and she punched it into her phone. A moment later, his phone trilled in his pocket, and when he checked it, her text was there with a kissy-face emoji. He wished he dared take her up on the suggestion, but she was probably joking.

He tucked the phone back into his pocket and rocked on his heels. "Are you free tomorrow? I'd like to take you out to lunch at this awesome place in Grand Central Station."

"I'd like that," she said with a nod. "Text me in the morning."

"I will," he said, then took two steps back, letting her know that he wouldn't keep her longer.

She put her key in the door, smiled over her shoulder, and went inside.

Mark quickly typed his first text to Dani. It consisted of one thing: the same emoji of a kissing smiley face. *He* wasn't kidding.

He hurried to work, walking with fast strides down the increasingly crowded sidewalk to reach the subway in time to catch the right train. Not once did he think about dealing with Andre; all of his thoughts were focused on Dani and how he could possibly convince her to stay in the city long enough to give both her career and him a real chance.

Chapter Six

Over the next week, Dani saw Mark every day for at least an hour or two—and often for a lot longer than that. One day they went to the Statue of Liberty and then to the 9/11 Memorial. On another, they got up really early and managed to be part of the crowd outside the *Today* show at Rockefeller Center. Dani got to shake Al Roker's hand. Then they wandered around Rock Center, taking it all in. Mark bought her a *Seinfeld* poster of Kramer that completely cracked her up.

As the days wore on, she crossed more and more things off her first-and-last list: browsing in Tiffany's, even though she could never afford anything in there. Being in the studio audience of a *Tonight Show* taping. Mark took her to a few places she'd never even heard of. In addition to the place he'd already promised in Grand Central—where he'd insisted she try some oyster dish—he brought her to The View, a restaurant at the top of a skyscraper, so high that on the way up in the glass elevator, her ears popped. Inside, the tables were on a carpeted ring that slowly rotated—one full circle every hour. Between trips to the buffet, patrons could look out and spot various landmarks, like the Chrysler building.

Every day, they laughed and talked. Some days, they busked—Dani enjoyed it more now, even after becoming aware of the audience. She'd taken to singing as well as dancing, and sometimes

Mark sang along, harmonizing with her. They used the proceeds to pay for dinner, a meal they shared almost every night now that Mark had been fired from yet another job. He swore he'd get another one soon, but he didn't want to miss out on their little remaining time together.

At times, she considered staying in Manhattan after all; if she could be this happy all the time, why wouldn't she? Except for the fact that the only reason Mark was being so nice was because their relationship, such as it was, had an expiration date.

If she were to stay, her life wouldn't be a constant stream of experiencing new things with Mark at her side. Eventually, they would both return to reality. He'd return to temp jobs and auditions. He wouldn't have time to hang out with her. And she'd be right where she'd been the day they met: alone penniless, rejected, and eventually, heading home to Pekin. What was the point of delaying the inevitable?

As great as the last week and a half had been, and as happy as Dani felt to be crossing items off her list, she couldn't help but notice with regret how close her departure date was drawing. Every night, she took her wall calendar off its nail and wrote down that day's activities. Then she counted the boxes left until she headed home.

They were vanishing awfully fast.

Worse, Mark seemed determined to bring up the fact that technically, she didn't have to leave. And he did so every time they said good night.

"It's only the cost of a flight," he said more than once.

Other times it was along the lines of, "You haven't sold your lease. You still have a place to live."

Or, "Come on. Give your career another shot."

Dani always brushed off whichever version he'd used. Her mother's daily emails and calls had beaten her down enough. She'd already started imagining her life back at home, maybe using her degree to teach high-school theater or something.

At her apartment door, she always gave him a long hug—their hugs were growing longer every night. She wanted to give him more than a hug, but that would be asking for trouble. Getting her emotions mixed up in something temporary—more than they already were—would be a mess.

On Monday, her last night in Manhattan, they walked back to her place extra slowly. They'd gotten into the habit of having Mark walk with her up to the apartment door, where they'd chat until he insisted she needed her sleep and then, of course, make another argument for why she should stay. Often as they leaned their backs against the wall, they'd end up sliding to the floor and sitting there talking for far longer than they should have.

As much as Dani loved sharing her first-and-last list with Mark, she'd come to enjoy their talks even more, except for how they always ended. That night, as they walked up the last flight of stairs, she dreaded having a final debate with him on what she wanted to be a magical conclusion to this part of her life. She still held her keys after using them on the front door. She hadn't put them back into her purse, because she didn't know if he'd want to talk about art and books when they both knew this was their last evening together.

Just as she'd feared, when they reached her door, he didn't strike up a conversation about music or movies or anything else they normally talked about. Instead, he grew quiet, as if he'd run out of things to say even about the Broadway show they'd just come from. She gripped her keys in one hand. A metal edge dug into her palm. The pain provided a distraction from the ache in her heart.

He didn't have to say why neither of them was talking; they both knew. They'd had a final day of adventures, and this was their last goodnight. She'd already packed her two suitcases, and all that remained to pack was her carryon. Last week, she'd shipped home a few boxes filled with things she'd collected in the last six months that hadn't fit into her bags.

As she stood at her door, she could picture the suitcases her mother had bought her for Christmas, which were bright red so they'd be easy to spot on the luggage carousel. They represented her failure here in the city and a dull, lifeless future.

Mom should have bought gray.

Mark stepped closer, and then closer again. She could feel the heat of his body, and her heart staccato-ed.

The image of those blasted suitcases forced themselves into her mind again. They marked the end of what could have been a wonderful thing with Mark.

No, not what could have been. What had been wonderful.

Eyes burning and insides tightening, she ordered herself to hold back her emotions. *Don't cry. I can still text Mark from four states and one time zone away. I can still email and call.*

But what were the chances a long-distance relationship would survive, when their time in person had existed for a matter of days? When both of them had purposely kept a slight, if deliberate, distance between them? It was as if they'd both instinctively known what *could* have been.

Now, with her head lowered, she watched as he took both of her hands in his. The keys tumbled from her grip back into her purse. He'd moved so close that she could feel his breath on her cheek. She knew without any doubt that if she looked up at him, their lips would meet. A kiss would be inevitable.

And oh, how she wanted that very thing. But two weeks from now, would she regret having kissed him, when she was home, driving past corn fields instead of exploring Times Square?

"You're trembling," Mark said, his voice soft, tender. He released one hand and cupped her face as he'd done before, but this time his thumb stroked her cheek. It was almost too much to bear. It felt so good, it hurt.

"Why did I have to meet you at the *end*?" she said quietly, still looking down. Seeing his face would break her. "Why not in January, when things could have been different?"

He didn't answer, as if he was waiting for her to act or speak. After several seconds of silence, she finally lifted her face to his, if only to wait for him to speak. In spite of her efforts, a tear escaped and trickled down her cheek. "And please don't say that I could still—"

He stopped her words by pressing his lips to hers, cradling her head between his hands with a sense of urgency.

A rush of heat went through Dani. She couldn't help but reach up and hold his face in return, kissing him back as much as she'd wanted to every day they'd been together. She poured all of her wishes and dreams into that kiss, and he returned every bit of it.

At last they broke apart, and Dani rested her cheek against his shoulder, catching her breath. Half of her wondered what kind of awful thing she'd done. The other half wanted to explode with happiness because even though she was leaving, at least she'd had that kiss.

She could feel Mark's heart pounding in his chest and knew that if she didn't get through her apartment door soon, she'd want to kiss him again and again and—

"I—I have to go," she murmured, gently pushing away. She didn't want to release her hands from his chest to let him go, but she forced herself to and somehow got the key into the lock.

She opened the door, went inside, and looked back at Mark. He had his hands in his pockets, and his expression looked as forlorn and lost as she felt.

"Thank you for everything," she whispered, and closed the door.

Chapter Seven

That night, Dani hardly slept; she stared at the ceiling. At her now-empty dresser. At her ugly red suitcases. At the window, where she gazed and imagined Mark sleeping in his apartment in the distance. She managed a couple of hours of unsettled sleep and woke an hour before her alarm.

She got up, ate a granola bar, and took a shower. She didn't have the heart to work on her appearance. What did it matter now? She pulled her hair into a ponytail and applied only the barest amount of makeup—a little concealer under her eyes so her parents wouldn't worry about her health, and some mascara, for the same reason; she tended to look extra tired without it.

Trying not to think of the kiss from last night—but reliving it every few minutes anyway—she finished packing up her carryon. She strapped the two suitcases together, the smaller atop the larger, and shouldered her carryon and purse. On the way to the door, she left her key on the counter next to the fridge, looked back at her three sleeping roommates—women she hardly knew even after six months—and walked out, rolling her luggage behind her.

The apartment door clanged shut and echoed against the apartment corridor as Dani made her way past the very spot where Mark had kissed her. Where she'd kissed him back.

At the elevator, she pushed the button, then, as she waited for it to arrive, she couldn't help but turn and look back at where she'd last seen Mark. Each of his arguments seemed to clamor in her mind, yelling at her all at once. Accusing her of abandoning her dreams. Of giving in to her mother's cynicism and insistence on a traditional role.

Of not giving us a real chance.

If they'd met even two months ago—one month ago?— things might have been different. If they'd met before she'd given her all and failed. Before she'd lost the spark that her childhood dreams had once given her. The spark wasn't dead, but it had dimmed an awful lot in six months.

The elevator dinged, and the door opened. She pulled her luggage inside, punched the button for the lobby, and leaned against the wall, closing her eyes and wishing she could rewind time enough to relive the last week and a half she'd spent with Mark. Better yet, to go back further and try to find him earlier. To do . . . *something* that would change the inevitable outcome of two strangers meeting, only to find a spark that had no hope of lasting.

Before stepping off the elevator, she instinctively reached for her pocket to check for her phone, and with the habitual act came a rush of memories: her first text to Mark, his reciprocal kissy face in return.

Their actual kiss last night.

She pulled her phone out and stared at it, trying to decide whether to send him one last text before she caught a taxi and headed for the airport. But the memory of Mark's devastated face, his desperate kiss filled with emotion, made her slip the phone back into her pocket. Mark was probably asleep—and sleeping well. She'd treated him poorly. Of course he'd be angry. He'd spent a lot of time with her. He'd spent what money he had on her. And now she was walking away. He had every right to be angry, even though she'd told him on their very first day that she wouldn't be here long.

The wheels of her luggage clicked on the seams of the lobby's tile but then stopped as her step slowed before the doors. She didn't *want* to leave. The last ten days had made New York feel like home in a way it never had in the previous weeks and months.

She'd miss everything about it, from the steam rising from the subway vents in the colder months to the heat radiating off the asphalt in the summer. The sheer energy everyone and everything exuded. The knowledge that people had walked this ground for centuries before her—many in the early years of the last century as they looked for a new life as they passed through Ellis Island.

She'd come here looking for a better life too—or at least, a different one. The day she'd headed for the Met, she'd been certain that after a few weeks back home, she'd be perfectly content to stay in the Midwest with her family. Perhaps she'd do community theater productions at times, just to scratch the itch. That would be enough. Or so she'd thought.

Go, or you'll miss your flight, she ordered herself.

Somehow that thought got her feet moving again, but as she reached for the door, her phone vibrated in her pocket. She paused and stepped back, pulling it out.

It was from Mark. A kissy face, with the words, *Have a good flight.*

Dani looked at the emoji for what felt like a long time, until it got blurry from unshed tears, and she finally slipped her phone back into her pocket. He might as well have said, *Have a good life.* They both knew it was over.

Not trusting herself to keep her tears at bay, she wiped at her eyes to dry them completely then headed for the doors again. This time she pushed the automatic button, and the door slowly swung open on its own. She walked outside into the dim morning of Manhattan. Everything seemed gray, and though it was probably just the early morning light filtering through the buildings, it seemed like a reflection of her inner state—gray and dreary. But, unlike the city, her state wouldn't change as the minutes ticked by with the dawn, bringing the sun with it.

Dani went to the curb and raised her arm to call a taxi. But a deep voice called out to her. "Going to the museum today?"

She whirled around to see Mark standing outside her building. She'd walked right past him. Her mind refused to work. "How long have you—what are you doing—why —" Her voice cut off as he stepped closer. He had rings under his eyes; her brow furrowed. "Have you been here all night?"

He shook his head, and she realized he wasn't wearing the same clothes as before. Silly of her to think he'd be out here waiting all night long. Her mom was right; her head was stuffed with cotton.

"I went back to my place, but I couldn't sleep. I've been here since about four didn't want to miss saying goodbye . . . for real."

Her eyes stung at that—their goodbye, their last words last night, weren't a good way to part.

But that kiss . . .

She looked at her watch; it was time to go if she was going to make her flight. "Mark, I have to—"

"No." He shook his head once and stepped closer. "Don't." Like last night, only slower, softer, he took her face between both of his hands. She tilted her head back and gazed into his eyes, lost in the moment and forgetting about JFK and her flight entirely, at least for now.

He looked into her eyes and raised his brows as if asking for permission. When her eyes lowered to his lips, he took that as an answer—which it was—and closed the distance. He kissed her slowly at first, and then deeper.

When he pulled back—too soon—he rested his forehead against hers. Dani's breath was uneven, and her legs trembled. She couldn't have held a solid relevé if her life depended on it. But slowly the world stopped spinning, and reality settled again.

"We've been through this," she began.

"But you haven't ever listened," Mark countered. She opened her mouth to protest, but he shook his head. "You once asked me why I keep chasing this crazy dream when I'm no closer to it now than I was six years ago."

Dani cocked her head. This wasn't the direction she'd expected the conversation to go.

Mark's face was intent. "I wasn't sure how to answer you then, but I spent all night thinking about it, and here's the truth: Dreams aren't worth chasing just for fame and fortune—and I know you said that you didn't come here hoping to get rich or famous. But you forgot what about dance brings you joy. It's the *journey* that matters as much as anything. I love music. You love dance. Artists. That's simply who we are. It's in our bones. And no, it's not practical. And yes, it's full of rejection and hard times and poverty too. But without those lows, we'd never get to soar in the amazing highs, either."

A dawning of understanding came over Dani. "Like when we first busked in the park." She'd found the joy of dance again in those few moments. Pure, unadulterated joy that had had nothing to do with what a casting director was looking for.

"We're two of a kind, Dani. You understand me. I understand you. Don't say it's not true, because it is. And in more ways than other artists understand each other. We have something special, something that can grow and become . . ."

"Become what?" Dani whispered the words. A tiny seed of hope was sprouting inside her, but fear threatened to quash it.

"Become something amazing." Mark took her hand and caressed the top with his thumb. "I'm not ready to give you up. And I think you're not ready to go back home, either."

She looked up at the fifth floor, where she'd spent so many nights. "But it's so *hard.*"

"I know," he said.

"What if neither of us ever makes it?" Dani didn't realize until the words were out of her mouth that she'd almost agreed to stay. The idea was growing larger in her mind.

"Then we'll take turns waiting tables and working as cashiers and taking tickets. Maybe we can start up a wedding DJ company to pay the bills between auditions. And we can go to the park and spend days busking just to buy a couple of amazing hot dogs and tickets to a play. I don't know all the answers, but I have to believe that we'll figure them out along the way if we give us a shot. Even if we work out but the music and dance don't—that would be worth it. And I can't help but think that no matter how miserable all of the hard parts will be, they'll be easier if you're there going through them with me."

Dani imagined coming off a horrible audition, knowing that Mark would be there to hold her and kiss her, then make her laugh, and make sure she had a raspberry smoothie.

So much better than sitting on my bed with a pint of ice cream.

Maybe she could face rejection for longer—a lot longer—if he was with her the whole way.

She threaded the fingers of both hands through his and stepped closer. "I don't think we ever did see the African collection, did we?"

Mark's mouth slowly curved in to a wide smile, and his eyes lit up. "Or the Costume Institute, either."

"Hmm. Weren't you going to take me to Chinatown? I think we've got a lot of things you still need to make good on, and that'll take a long time. Months, probably. Maybe years." She was unable to maintain the banter when her insides were ready to burst.

He brushed a strand of hair from her face. "Years," he said. "Definitely."

A Note to the Reader

I hope you enjoyed reading *Firsts and Lasts* as much as I enjoyed writing it, especially tapping into my own visit to New York. I made sure to pass it along to my dear friend and fellow writer Luisa Perkins, as she lived in New York for many years, and caught several things a tourist like me wouldn't know.

I love feedback! So tell me: What did you like? What did you love? What didn't you like so much? Do you have a great idea for theme, location, or time period for a future novel or novella?

Write to let me know! You can reach me at
annette@annettelyon.com

To hear about my upcoming releases, events, and sales, be sure to sign up for my newsletter on my website.

Finally, if you're so inclined, it would be wonderful if you left a review for *Firsts and Lasts*. I appreciate all feedback, and reviews do so much in helping other readers find the kinds of books they'll enjoy.

Thanks again for spending time with Dani and Mark!

With gratitude,

Annette Lyon

About the Author

Annette Lyon is a *USA Today* bestselling author, a five-time Best of State medalist for fiction in Utah, and a Whitney Award winner. She's had success as a professional editor and in newspaper, magazine, and technical writing, but her first love has always been writing fiction.

She's a cum laude graduate from BYU with a degree in English and is the author of over a dozen books, including the Whitney Award-winning *Band of Sisters*, a chocolate cookbook, and a grammar guide. She is a regular contributor to and the former editor of the *Timeless Romance Anthology* series. She has received five publication awards from the League of Utah Writers, including the Silver Quill, and she's one of the four coauthors of the *Newport Ladies Book Club* series. Annette is represented by Heather Karpas at ICM Partners.

To receive updates on sales, new releases, and events, sign up for her newsletter by scanning the code below.

And to find more of her work on her Amazon author page, scan this code:

www.ingramcontent.com/pod-product-compliance
Lightning Source LLC
Chambersburg PA
CBHW071629140626
46555CB00021B/1756